to:

This book is on loan from
Library Services for Schools

Cumbria
County Council

PRESS THE PAGE
HEAR THE NOISE!

LITTLE TIGER PRESS
An imprint of Magi Publications
1 The Coda Centre, 189 Munster Road, London SW6 6AW
www.littletigerpress.com

First published in Great Britain 2011

Text copyright © Magi Publications 2011
Illustrations copyright © Daniel Howarth 2011

Daniel Howarth has asserted his right to be identified as the illustrator
of this work under the Copyright, Designs and Patent Act, 1988

A CIP catalogue record for this book is
available from the British Library

All rights reserved • ISBN 978-1-84895-230-0

Printed in China • LTP/1800/0213/0511

2 4 6 8 10 9 7 5 3 1

Old MacDonald had a Farm

Illustrated by Daniel Howarth

LITTLE TIGER PRESS
London

Old MacDonald had a farm,
E-I-E-I-O!
And on that farm he had some sheep,
E-I-E-I-O!

"Come on, sheep! You should be in the pen."

With a *BAAA! BAAA!* here,
And a *BAAA! BAAA!* there . . .

"Oh, you cheeky sheep!"

. . . Here a *BAAA!*
There a *BAAA!*
Everywhere a *BAAA! BAAA!*
Old MacDonald had a farm,
E-I-E-I-O!

Baaa!

Baaa!

"Into the barn you go.
Heave!"

Old MacDonald had a farm,
E-I-E-I-O!
And on that farm
he had some cows,
E-I-E-I-O!
With a *MOO! MOO!* here,
And a *MOO! MOO!* there . . .

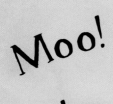

Moo!

Moo!

Moo!
Moo!

. . . Here a *MOO!*
There a *MOO!*
Everywhere a *MOO! MOO!*
Old MacDonald had a farm,
E-I-E-I-O!

Old MacDonald had a farm,
E-I-E-I-O!
And on that farm he had some pigs,
E-I-E-I-O!
With an *OINK! OINK!* here,
And an *OINK! OINK!* there . . .

Oink!

Oink!

Old MacDonald had a farm,
E-I-E-I-O!
And on that farm he had some ducks,
E-I-E-I-O!
With a *QUACK! QUACK!* here,
And a *QUACK! QUACK!* there . . .

"I'm soaking wet!"

. . . Here a *QUACK!*
There a *QUACK!*
Everywhere a *QUACK! QUACK!*
Old MacDonald had a farm,
E-I-E-I-O!

Quack!

Quack!

"Will those naughty animals ever behave?"

Old MacDonald had a farm,
E-I-E-I-O!
And on that farm he had a dog,
E-I-E-I-O!
With a *WOOF! WOOF!* here,
And a *WOOF! WOOF!* there . . .

Woof!
Woof!

YOU CAN'T MISS THESE VERY NOISY PICTURE BOOKS!

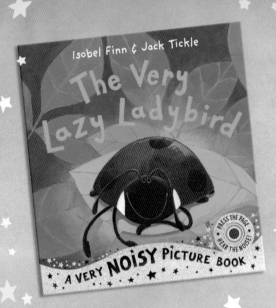

Isobel Finn & Jack Tickle

The Very Lazy Ladybird

A VERY NOISY PICTURE BOOK

The Wheels on the Bus

A VERY NOISY PICTURE BOOK

WHAT'S THAT NOISE, LITTLE MOUSE?

Stephanie Stansbie
Polona Lovsin

A VERY NOISY PICTURE BOOK

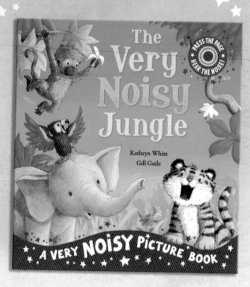

The Very Noisy Jungle

Kathryn White
Gill Guile

A VERY NOISY PICTURE BOOK

PRESS THE PAGE
HEAR THE NOISE!

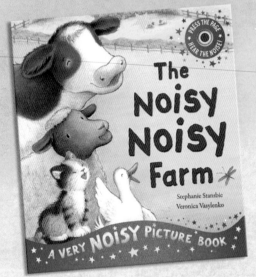

The Noisy Noisy Farm

Stephanie Stansbie
Veronica Vasylenko

A VERY NOISY PICTURE BOOK

PRESS THE PAGE
HEAR THE NOISE!

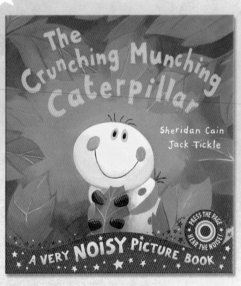

The Crunching Munching Caterpillar

Sheridan Cain
Jack Tickle

A VERY NOISY PICTURE BOOK

PRESS THE PAGE
HEAR THE NOISE!

For information regarding any of the above
titles or for our catalogue, please contact us:
Little Tiger Press, 1 The Coda Centre,
189 Munster Road, London SW6 6AW
E-mail: info@littletiger.co.uk • www.littletigerpress.com
Tel: 020 7385 6333 • Fax: 020 7385 7333